Chisa C. Evans

Doodleville Blues
Copyright © 2023 by Chisa C. Evans

All rights reserved. No part of this publication may be reproduced, distributed, or transmitted in any form or by any means, including photocopying, recording, or other electronic or mechanical methods, without the prior written permission of the author, except in the case of brief quotations embodied in critical reviews and certain other non-commercial uses permitted by copyright law.

Tellwell Talent
www.tellwell.ca

ISBN
978-0-2288-8588-7 (Hardcover)
978-0-2288-8589-4 (Paperback)

Once upon a time there lived a small doodle family in the great town of Doodleville.

There was daddy doodle Gabe, mommy doodle Cara, and their three little doodles. Aiden was the competitive little doodle. Gabby was the inquisitive little doodle. Alex, called "Squirt" because of his small stature, was the timid little doodle.

The doodle family lived inside a big blue house. There was a park with their very own rose garden. A water fountain splashed away in front of the rose garden and up the hill a family of blue birds lived inside a grand oak tree.

Every morning daddy and mommy doodle took the family on an adventure. They'd stop to smell the roses.

They'd run through the mist of the water fountain.

Then they would shake, shake, shake!
until their fur was fluffy and dry.

The blue bird family sang "Tra-la-la-la, twe-lee-lee!" The leaves went "swish, swish swish" in the tree.

Just beneath the grand oak tree were three mountains of leaves. Some were brown, some orange, some red and some green.

They were piled high for each doodle to dive into.

Competitive Aiden, with his tongue hanging in excitement, dove right in. Covered from head to paw, he rolled around with delight.

Next was inquisitive Gabby, but she had questions.

"Mommy, how high is this mountain?"

"How many leaves are there? One hundred or one thousand?"

"Do worms live in there?"

"Will I need a bath after?"

"Jump in and find out!" said mommy doodle with a smile.

Gabby loved the idea of being covered in fun, so she jumped in head first.

"Boy oh boy, am I glad I jumped in! What fun!"

She and Aiden shared a high paw.

Aiden and Gabby waved for Alex to join them.

Alex could feel the butterflies in his little doodle belly.

What if there are little critters inside the leaf mountain? he thought.

Caterpillars, ladybugs, grasshoppers and crickets were just a few of the fears that made his dreams so wicked.

Alex whimpered and quivered. He didn't want to jump in!

Daddy Gabe rushed to his side and said, "Be brave, my little doodle. There's nothing to fear."

Alex peeped through his paws at the mountain of leaves. Mommy doodle put her paw around him and said, "It's OK, darling doodle. You'll do it next time."

Alex smiled. Then, he ran as fast as he could to join the rest of his doodle family for lunch and more fun in the sun.

As the sun went down, they chased lightning bugs to their hearts' delight.

One lightning bug, two lightning bugs, three. Lightning bugs as far as the eye could see. They lit the way back to the big blue house.

In went Cara, in went Aiden, in went Gabby. But where's Alex?

He was afraid of the dark, so he covered his eyes and hid in the rose garden.

Not to worry, daddy doodle to the rescue!

Daddy doodle touched Alex's head and said, "Be brave, my big little doodle!"

Daddy doodle carried Alex into the big blue house.

The whole doodle family was safe and warm together. They slept soundly next to the warm fireplace.

Suddenly, the wind howled. The trees swayed.
Rain fell from the sky.

A loud clap of thunder sent Alex
running into an unfamiliar night.

He ran to the beautiful rose garden.
The roses drooped with the tears of the sky.

He ran to the water fountain that gave such joy.
But it ran over like a raging river.

The grand oak, where the blue birds lived, was the scariest of all.

Shadows chased him everywhere he turned.

He was so frightened! He covered his eyes and began to cry.

He felt alone, scared, and cold.
Most of all he missed his family!

He missed Mommy pulling him and
his siblings close to cuddle.

He missed daddy saying, "You are never
alone as long as we have each other."

He remembered playing tug of war with
Aiden and Gabby rolling over backwards
when Aiden pulled the rope away.

Then, he heard a voice as clear as the whiskers on his face: "Be brave, my big little doodle."

It was the last thing Daddy said to him before the storm.

The words made him feel like he could do anything.

Sunlight or rain, day or night.

He would be brave just like Daddy told him.

So he stood up off the cold, wet, grass.

He would face the scary things he saw.

He ran back to the grand oak tree. Nothing was chasing him at all. They were the shadows of the branches. He remembered the blue bird family singing "Tra-la-la-la, twe-lee-lee!"

He raced back to the water fountain. It wasn't a raging river! The overflow of rainwater was only trickling over the sides! He ran beneath the trickling water. Then he remembered to shake, shake, shake! himself fluffy and dry. Mommy would be so proud!

He galloped to the beautiful rose garden. The roses weren't so heavy with the sky's tears. They stood tall and proud just like before!

As he turned the corner, he saw a familiar sight.

Could it be?

Oh, how he hoped it would be.

Yes, it was the big blue house where he lived with his little doodle family!

Alex proudly marched to the house. He had conquered his fears of the backyard.

In the rain! At night! All by himself!

He couldn't wait to tell them all about his adventure.

He felt competitive like his brother. He felt inquisitive like his sister.

Most importantly, he felt fearless. He learned that he was brave, just as Daddy said!

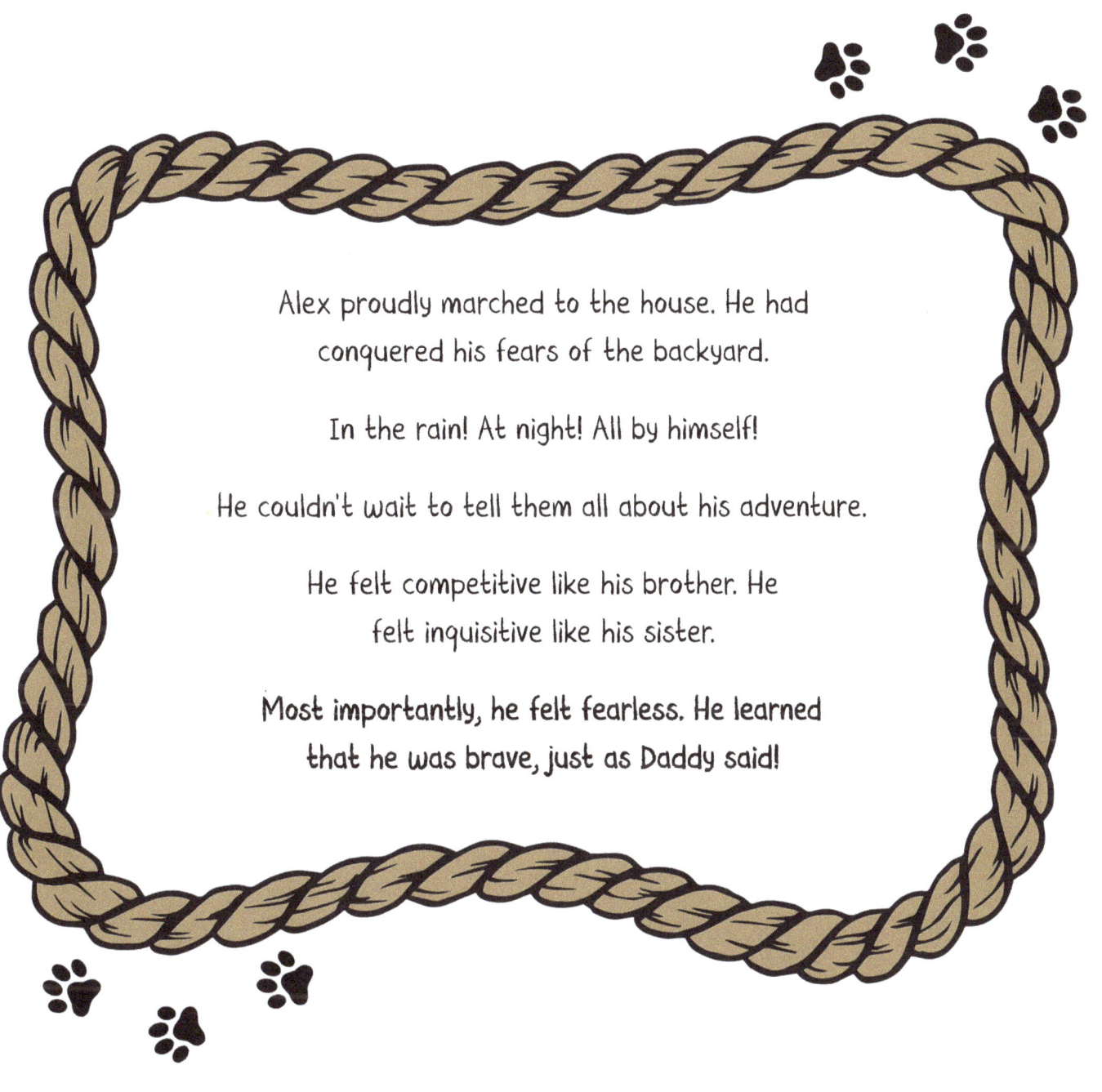

He darted through the doggy door.

He woke his siblings and told them the great things he saw. Aiden, Gabby, and Alex joined in a sibling high paw. Mommy Cara pulled him close to cuddle-oh how he missed her warmth! Then daddy Gabe put his arm around him and said, "You are my brave little doodle!"

"Why are your paws muddy, Daddy?" asked Alex.

"Remember what I told you son? You are never alone as long as we have each other", he lovingly answered.

Daddy doodle was there the whole time!

The entire doodle family shared a great big grand doodle hug.

"What's our next doodle adventure?" asked
Alex, his tail wagging uncontrollably.

Every doodle laughed and laughed.

And was ready to go.

About the Author

Chisa C. Evans was born and raised in Thomasville, Alabama. She is one of four siblings and comes from a fairly large family, so family has always and continues to be priority to her. That family includes her husband and her four-legged teddy bear pup "boys" that this book is loosely based. *Doodleville Blues* is Chisa's first children's book.

Because every great story has a true inspiration, meet Cole and Enzo, the real heartbeats of *Doodleville Blues*.

Printed in the USA
CPSIA information can be obtained
at www.ICGtesting.com
LVHW060956290124
770139LV00006B/225